The Orchestra Pit

JOHANNA WRIGHT

A NEAL PORTER BOOK

ROARING BROOK PRESS

NEW YORK

Copyright © 2014 by Johanna Wright
A Neal Porter Book
Published by Roaring Brook Press
Roaring Brook Press is a division of Holtzbrinck Publishing Holdings Limited Partnership
175 Fifth Avenue, New York, New York 10010
The art for this book was created using acrylic paint on canvas and black India ink for the outlines.
mackids.com

Library of Congress Cataloging-in-Publication Data
Wright, Johanna, author, illustrator.
    The orchestra pit / Johanna Wright. — First edition.
        pages cm
    "A Neal Porter Book."
    Summary: "When a slightly befuddled but surprisingly endearing snake
wanders into the wrong pit—the orchestra pit—peculiar things start to
happen"— Provided by publisher.
    ISBN 978-1-59643-769-2 (hardcover)
[1. Orchestra—Fiction. 2. Snakes—Fiction. 3. Jungle animals—Fiction.]
I. Title.
    PZ7.W9496Or 2014
    [E]—dc23
                                                            2013016729

Roaring Brook Press books may be purchased for business or promotional use. For information on bulk purchases
please contact Macmillan Corporate and Premium Sales Department at (800) 221-7945 x5442
or by email at specialmarkets@macmillan.com.

First edition 2014
Book design by Jennifer Browne
Printed in China by Toppan Leefung Printing Ltd., Dongguan City, Guangdong Province

1   3   5   7   9   10   8   6   4   2

For Cooper
and Namju

I have a feeling

I'm in the wrong pit.

The orchestra pit!

It's time to do a bit of exploring.

That trumpet
is LOUD!

The tuba
is quite
roomy.

The trombone
is almost as long
as I am.

Bonjour,
French horn.

Something must have
startled them . . .

Here are the wind instruments.

The flute

The clarinet

The piccolo

The bassoon

That oboe is rather charming.

The string section seems friendlier.

The violin

The viola

The cello

And I'm quite attached
to the bass.

Uh-oh!

Time to hide.

Is that an elephant
I hear?

A hippo?

A bird?

The strings remind me
of monkeys.

The percussion sounds like a gorilla.

It's about to begin.

Quiet . . .

Loud!

What a racket!

Time to head home.

Out of the wrong pit . . .

And into . . .

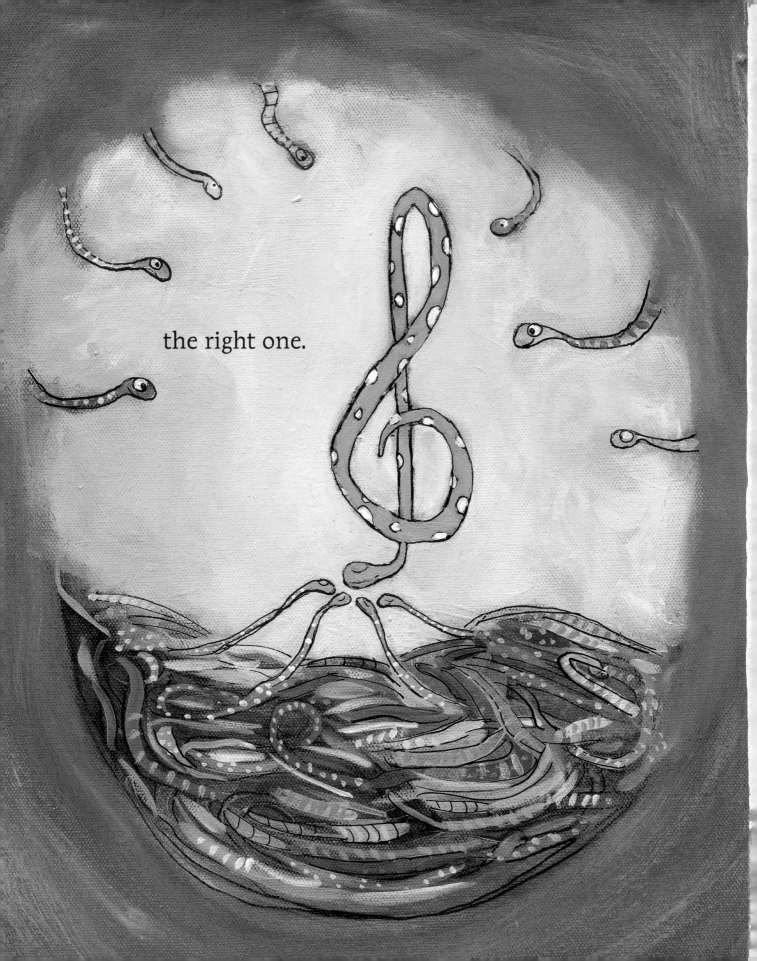